AN EXPOTITION
TO THE
NORTH POLE

AN EXPOTITION
TO THE
NORTH POLE

A.A. MILNE

illustrated by

ERNEST H. SHEPARD

One fine day Pooh had stumped up to the top of the Forest to see if his friend Christopher Robin was interested in Bears at all. At breakfast that morning (a simple meal of marmalade spread lightly over a honeycomb or two) he had suddenly thought of a new song. It began like this:

'Sing Ho! for the life of a Bear.'

When he had got as far as this, he scratched his head, and thought to himself, 'That's a very good start for a song, but what about the second line?' He tried singing 'Ho,' two or three times, but it didn't

 seem to help. 'Perhaps it would be better,' he thought, 'if I sang Hi for the life of a Bear.' So he sang it . . . but it wasn't.

'Very well, then, he said, 'I shall sing
that first line twice, and perhaps if I sing
it very quickly, I shall find myself singing
the third and fourth lines before I have
time to think of them, and that will be a
Good Song. Now then:

     Sing Ho! for the life of a Bear!
     Sing Ho! for the life of a Bear!
I don't much mind if it rains or snows,
'Cos I've got a lot of honey on my nice new nose!
I don't much care if it snows or thaws,
'Cos I've got a lot of honey on my nice clean paws!
     Sing Ho! for a Bear!
     Sing Ho! for a Pooh!
And I'll have a little something in an hour or two!

He was so pleased with this song that
he sang it all the way to the top of the
Forest, 'and if I go on singing it much
longer,' he thought, 'it will be time for
the little something, and then the last

line won't be true.' So he turned it into a hum instead.

Christopher Robin was sitting outside his door, putting on his Big Boots. As soon as he saw the Big Boots, Pooh knew that an Adventure was going to happen, and he brushed the honey off his nose with the back of his paw, and spruced himself up as well as he could, so as to look Ready for Anything.

'Good morning, Christopher Robin,' he called out.

'Hallo, Pooh Bear. I can't get this boot on.'

'That's bad,' said Pooh.

'Do you think you could very kindly lean against me, 'cos I keep pulling so hard that I fall over backwards.'

Pooh sat down, dug his feet into the ground, and pushed hard against Christopher Robin's back, and Christopher Robin pushed hard against his, and pulled and pulled at his boot until he had got it on.

'And that's that,' said Pooh. 'What do we do next?'

'We are all going on an Expedition,' said Christopher Robin, as he got up and brushed himself. 'Thank you, Pooh.'

'Going on an Expotition?' said Pooh eagerly. 'I don't think I've ever been on one of those. Where are we going to on this Expotition?'

'Expedition, silly old Bear. It's got an "x" in it.'

'Oh!' said Pooh. 'I know.' But he didn't really.

'We're going to discover the North Pole.'

'Oh!' said Pooh again. 'What *is* the North Pole?' he asked.

'It's just a thing you discover,' said Christopher Robin carelessly, not being quite sure himself.

'Oh! I see,' said Pooh. 'Are bears any good at discovering it?'

'Of course they are. And Rabbit and Kanga and all of you. It's an Expedition. That's what an Expedition means. A long line of everybody. You'd better tell the others to get ready, while I see if my gun's all right. And we must all bring Provisions.'

'Bring what?'

'Things to eat.'

'Oh!' said Pooh happily. 'I thought you said Provisions. I'll go and tell them.' And he stumped off.

The first person he met was Rabbit.

'Hallo, Rabbit,' he said, 'is that you?'

'Let's pretend it isn't,' said Rabbit, 'and see what happens.'

'I've got a message for you.'

'I'll give it to him.'

'We're all going on an Expotition with Christopher Robin!'

'What is it when we're on it?'

'A sort of boat, I think,' said Pooh.
'Oh! that sort.'

'Yes. And we're going to discover
a Pole or something. Or was it a
Mole? Anyhow we're going to discover it.'

'We are, are we?' said Rabbit.

'Yes. And we've got to bring Pro—
things to eat with us. In case we want
to eat them. Now I'm going down to
Piglet's. Tell Kanga, will you?'

He left Rabbit and hurried down to Piglet's house. The Piglet was sitting on the ground at the door of his house blowing happily at a dandelion, and wondering whether it would be this year, next year, sometime, or never. He had just discovered that it would be never, and was trying to remember what '*it*' was, and hoping it wasn't anything nice, when Pooh came up.

'Oh! Piglet,' said Pooh excitedly, 'we're going on an Expotition, all of us, with things to eat. To discover something.'

'To discover what?' said Piglet anxiously.

'Oh! just something.'

'Nothing fierce?'

'Christopher Robin didn't say anything about fierce. He just said it had an "x".'

'It isn't their necks I mind,' said Piglet earnestly. 'It's their teeth. But if Christopher Robin is coming I don't mind anything.'

In a little while they were all ready at the top of the Forest, and the Expotition started. First came Christopher Robin and Rabbit, then Piglet and Pooh; then Kanga, with Roo in her pocket, and Owl; then Eeyore; and, at the end, in a long line, all Rabbit's friends-and-relations.

'I didn't ask them,' explained Rabbit carelessly. 'They just came. They always

do. They can march at the end, after Eeyore.'

'What I say,' said Eeyore, 'is that it's unsettling. I didn't want to come on this Expo – what Pooh said. I only came to oblige. But here I am; and if I am the end of the Expo – what we're talking about – then let me *be* the end. But if, every time I want to sit down for a little rest, I have to brush away half a dozen of Rabbit's smaller friends-and-relations first, then this isn't an Expo – whatever it is – at all, it's simply a Confused Noise. That's what *I* say.'

'I see what Eeyore means,' said Owl. 'If you ask me—'

'I'm not asking anybody,' said Eeyore. 'I'm just telling everybody. We can look for the North Pole, or we can play "Here we go gathering Nuts and May" with the end part of an ants' nest. It's all the same to me.'

There was a shout from the top of the line.

'Come on!' called Christopher Robin.

'Come on!' called Pooh and Piglet.

'Come on!' called Owl.

'We're starting,' said Rabbit. 'I must go.' And he hurried off to the front of the Expotition with Christopher Robin.

'All right,' said Eeyore. 'We're going. Only Don't Blame Me.'

So off they all went to discover the Pole.

And as they walked, they chattered
to each other of this and that, all except
Pooh, who was making up a song.

'This is the first verse,' he said to
Piglet, when he was ready with it.

'First verse of what?'

'My song.'

'What song?'

'This one.'

'Which one?'

'Well, if you listen, Piglet, you'll hear it.'

'How do you know I'm not listening?'

Pooh couldn't answer that one, so he
began to sing.

They all went off to discover the Pole,
   Owl and Piglet and Rabbit and all;
It's a Thing you Discover, as I've been tole
   By Owl and Piglet and Rabbit and all.
Eeyore, Christopher Robin and Pooh
And Rabbit's relations all went too –
And where the Pole was none of them knew. . . .
   Sing Hey! for Owl and Rabbit and all!

'Hush!' said Christopher Robin, turning
round to Pooh, 'we're just coming to
a Dangerous Place.'

'Hush!' said Pooh, turning round
quickly to Piglet.

'Hush!' said Piglet to Kanga.

'Hush!' said Kanga to Owl, while Roo
said 'Hush!' several times to himself
very quietly.

'Hush!' said Owl to Eeyore.

'*Hush!*' said Eeyore in a terrible voice
to all Rabbit's friends-and-relations, and
'Hush!' they said hastily to each other
all down the line, until it got to the last
one of all. And the last and smallest
friend-and-relation was so upset to find
that the whole Expotition was saying 'Hush!'
to *him*, that he buried himself head down-
wards in a crack in the ground, and stayed
there for two
days until
the danger was
over, and then
went home in
a great hurry,
and lived quietly with his Aunt ever-
afterwards. His name was Alexander Beetle.

They had come to a stream which twisted
and tumbled between high rocky banks,
and Christopher Robin saw at once how
dangerous it was.

'It's just the place,' he explained,
'for an Ambush.'

'What sort of bush?' whispered Pooh to
Piglet. 'A gorse-bush?'

'My dear Pooh,' said Owl in his superior
way, 'don't you know what an Ambush is?'

'Owl,' said Piglet, looking round at him
severely, 'Pooh's whisper was a perfectly
private whisper, and there was no need—'

'An Ambush,' said Owl, 'is a sort of
Surprise.'

'So is a gorse-bush sometimes,' said Pooh.

'An Ambush, as I was about to explain
to Pooh,' said Piglet, 'is a sort of
Surprise.'

'If people jump out at you suddenly,
that's an Ambush,' said Owl.

'It's an Ambush, Pooh, when people jump
at you suddenly,' explained Piglet.

Pooh, who now knew what an Ambush was,
said that a gorse-bush had sprung at him
suddenly one day when he fell off a tree,

and he had taken six days to get all the prickles out of himself.

'We are not *talking* about gorse-bushes,' said Owl a little crossly.

'I am,' said Pooh.

They were climbing very cautiously up the stream now, going from rock to rock, and after they had gone a little way they came to a place where the banks widened out at each side, so that on each side of the water there was a level strip of grass on which they could sit down and rest. As soon as he saw this, Christopher Robin called 'Halt!' and they all sat down and rested.

'I think,' said Christopher Robin, 'that we ought to eat all our Provisions now, so that we shan't have so much to carry.'

'Eat all our what?' said Pooh.

'All that we've brought,' said Piglet, getting to work.

'That's a good idea,' said Pooh, and he got to work too.

'Have you all got something?' asked
Christopher Robin with his mouth full.

'All except me,' said Eeyore. 'As Usual.'
He looked round at them in his melancholy
way. 'I suppose none of you are sitting on
a thistle by any chance?'

'I believe I am,' said Pooh. 'Ow!' He
got up, and looked behind him. 'Yes, I was.
I thought so.'

'Thank you, Pooh. If you've quite finished
with it.' He moved across to Pooh's place,
and began to eat.

'It doesn't do them any Good, you know,
sitting on them,' he went on, as he looked

up munching. 'Takes all the Life out of them. Remember that another time, all of you. A little Consideration, a little Thought for Others, makes all the difference.'

As soon as he had finished his lunch Christopher Robin whispered to Rabbit, and Rabbit said, 'Yes, yes, of course,' and they walked a little way up the stream together.

'I don't want the others to hear,' said Christopher Robin.

'Quite so,' said Rabbit, looking important.

'It's – I wondered – It's only – Rabbit, I suppose *you* don't know. What does the North Pole *look* like?'

'Well,' said Rabbit, stroking his whiskers. 'Now you're asking me.'

'I did know once, only I've sort of forgotten,' said Christopher Robin carelessly.

'It's a funny thing,' said Rabbit, 'but I've sort of forgotten too, although I did know *once*.'

'I suppose it's just a pole stuck in the ground.'

'Sure to be a pole,' said Rabbit, 'because of calling it a pole, and if it's a pole, well, I should think it would be sticking in the ground, shouldn't you, because there'd be nowhere else to stick it.'

'Yes, that's what I thought.'

'The only thing,' said Rabbit, 'is, *where is it sticking*?'

'That's what we're looking for,' said Christopher Robin.

They went back to the others. Piglet was lying on his back, sleeping peacefully. Roo was washing his face and paws in the stream, while Kanga explained to everybody proudly that this was the first time he had ever washed his face himself, and Owl was telling Kanga an Interesting Anecdote full of long words like Encyclopaedia and Rhododendron to which Kanga wasn't listening.

'I don't hold with all this washing,' grumbled Eeyore. 'This modern Behind-the-ears nonsense. What do *you* think, Pooh?'

'Well,' said Pooh, '*I* think—'

But we shall never know what Pooh thought, for there came a sudden squeak from Roo, a splash, and a loud cry of alarm from Kanga.

'So much for *washing*,' said Eeyore.

'Roo's fallen in!' cried Rabbit, and he and Christopher Robin came rushing down to the rescue.

'Look at me swimming!' squeaked Roo from
the middle of his pool, and was hurried
down a waterfall into the next pool.

'Are you all right, Roo, dear?' called
Kanga anxiously.

'Yes!' said Roo. 'Look at me sw—' and
down he went over the next waterfall into
another pool.

Everybody was doing something to help.
Piglet, wide awake suddenly, was jumping
up and down and making 'Oo, I say' noises;
Owl was explaining that in a case of Sudden
and Temporary Immersion the Important
Thing was to keep the Head Above Water;
Kanga was jumping along the bank, saying
'Are you *sure* you're all right, Roo dear?'
to which Roo, from whatever pool he was in
at the moment, was answering 'Look at me
swimming!' Eeyore had turned round and
hung his tail over the first pool into which
Roo fell, and with his back to the accident
was grumbling quietly to himself, and saying,

'All this washing; but catch on to my tail, little Roo, and you'll be all right'; and Christopher Robin and Rabbit came hurrying past Eeyore, and were calling out to the others in front of them.

'All Right, Roo, I'm coming,' called Christopher Robin.

'Get something across the stream, lower down, some of you fellows,' called Rabbit.

But Pooh was getting something. Two pools below Roo he was standing with a long pole in his paws, and Kanga came up and took one end of it, and between them they held it across the lower part of the pool;

and Roo, still bubbling proudly, 'Look at me swimming,' drifted up against it, and climbed out.

'Did you see me swimming?' squeaked Roo excitedly, while Kanga scolded him and rubbed him down. 'Pooh, did you see me swimming? That's called swimming, what I was doing. Rabbit, did you see what I was doing? Swimming. Hallo, Piglet! I say, Piglet! What do you think I was doing! Swimming! Christopher Robin, did you see me—'

But Christopher Robin wasn't listening. He was looking at Pooh.

'Pooh,' he said, 'where did you find that pole?'

Pooh looked at the pole in his hands.

'I just found it,' he said. 'I thought it ought to be useful. I just picked it up.'

'Pooh,' said Christopher Robin solemnly, 'the Expedition is over. You have found the North Pole!'

'Oh!' said Pooh.

Eeyore was sitting with his tail in the
water when they all got back to him.

'Tell Roo to be quick, somebody,' he said.
'My tail's getting cold. I don't want to
mention it, but I just mention it. I don't
want to complain, but there it is. My
tail's cold.'

'Here I am!' squeaked Roo.

'Oh, there you are.'

'Did you see me swimming?'

Eeyore took his tail out of the water, and
swished it from side to side.

'As I expected,' he said. 'Lost all feeling.
Numbed it. That's what it's done.
Numbed it. Well, as long as nobody minds,
I suppose it's all right.'

'Poor old Eeyore! I'll dry it for you,'
said Christopher Robin, and he took out
his handkerchief and rubbed it up.

'Thank you, Christopher Robin. You're the
only one who seems to understand about
tails. They don't think – that's what's

the matter with some of these others.
They've no imagination. A tail isn't a
tail to *them*, it's just a Little Bit Extra
at the back.'

'Never mind, Eeyore,' said Christopher
Robin, rubbing his hardest. 'Is *that* better?'

'It's feeling more like a tail perhaps.
It Belongs again, if you know what I mean.'

'Hullo, Eeyore,' said Pooh, coming up to
them with his pole.

'Hullo, Pooh. Thank you for asking, but
I shall be able to use it again in a day
or two.'

'Use what?' said Pooh.

'What we are talking about.'

'I wasn't talking about anything,' said
Pooh, looking puzzled.

'My mistake again. I thought you were saying
how sorry you were about my tail, being all
numb, and could you do anything to help?'

'No,' said Pooh. 'That wasn't me,' he said.
He thought for a little and then suggested

helpfully: 'Perhaps it was somebody else.'

'Well, thank him for me when you see him.'

Pooh looked anxiously at Christopher Robin.

'Pooh's found the North Pole,' said Christopher Robin. 'Isn't that lovely?'

Pooh looked modestly down.

'Is that it?' said Eeyore.

'Yes,' said Christopher Robin.

'Is that what we were looking for?'

'Yes,' said Pooh.

'Oh!' said Eeyore. 'Well, anyhow – it didn't rain,' he said.

They stuck the pole in the ground, and Christopher Robin tied a message on to it:

NoRTH PoLE
DICSovERED By
PooH
PooH FouND IT

Then they all went home again. And I think, but I am not quite sure, that Roo had a hot bath and went straight to bed. But Pooh went back to his own house, and feeling very proud of what he had done, had a little something to revive himself.

An Expotition to the North Pole
is taken from *Winnie-the-Pooh*
originally published in
Great Britain 14 October 1926
by Methuen & Co. Ltd
Text by A.A. Milne and line drawings by Ernest H. Shepard
copyright under the Berne Convention

This book club edition published by Grolier 1995
Published by arrangement with Reed Children's Books

First published in this edition 1990
by Methuen Children's Books
an imprint of Reed Children's Books
Michelin House, 81 Fulham Road, London SW3 6RB
and Auckland, Melbourne, Singapore and Toronto
Reprinted 1991, 1992, 1994, 1995

Printed in Hong Kong

ISBN 0 416 16632 6